Too Many Ghosts!

by Frances Ann Ladd

Illustrated by Duendes del Sur

TM

SCHOLASTIC INC.

New York   Toronto   London   Auckland   Sydney
Mexico City   New Delhi   Hong Kong   Buenos Aires

It was a dark night.
"Look Scoob!
There is a ghost
at that house!
No, two ghosts!"
said Shaggy.
Scooby and Shaggy
hid behind some trees.
"There are
three witches, too!
That house
must be haunted."

"Jeepers!
All the houses
on the street
are haunted!"
said Shaggy.
The ghosts and witches
were holding bags.

Two ghosts came up
behind Shaggy.
"Boo!" said the ghosts.
Shaggy and Scooby
jumped.
"Zoinks!" Shaggy yelled.

The ghosts held out
their bags.
"Get those haunted bags
away from me!"
Shaggy yelled.

"Trick or treat,"
said the ghosts.
"Trick or treat?"
said Shaggy.
"It's Halloween,"
said one ghost.
"We are just kids,"
said the other.
"Oh! Like, we knew that!"
said Shaggy.

"Do you have
any candy?"
said one ghost.
"We don't want apples,"
the other ghost said.

"We have
Scooby Snacks,"
Shaggy said.
The ghosts looked mad.
"Dog food is a trick!
We want treats!"
said the ghosts.
More ghosts came over.
"Treats, treats, treats!"
said all the ghosts.

"Like, let's get out of here!"
Shaggy and Scooby ran away